I SPY
SCHOOL DAYS

A BOOK OF PICTURE RIDDLES

Photographs by **Walter Wick**
Riddles by **Jean Marzollo**

With new bonus challenges by
Dan Marzollo and **Dave Marzollo**

cartwheel books™

An imprint of Scholastic Inc.
New York

For my nieces, Heather, Jessica, and Emily,
and my nephews, David, Peter, and Michael
W.W.

For Marjorie Holderman, Joanne Marien, and
Gerrie Paige
J.M.

Book design by Carol Devine Carson

Text copyright © 1995 by Jean Marzollo
Photographs copyright © 1995 by Walter Wick
Bonus challenges copyright © 2021 by Dan Marzollo and Dave Marzollo
All rights reserved. Published by Scholastic Inc., *Publishers since 1920.* SCHOLASTIC, CARTWHEEL BOOKS, and
associated logos are trademarks and/or registered trademarks of Scholastic Inc. • The publisher does not have
any control over and does not assume any responsibility for author or third-party websites or their content. •
No part of this publication may be reproduced, stored in a retrieval system, or transmitted in any form or by
any means, electronic, mechanical, photocopying, recording, or otherwise, without written permission of the
publisher. For information regarding permission, write to Scholastic Inc., Attention: Permissions Department,
557 Broadway, New York, NY 10012.
Library of Congress Cataloging-in-Publication Data available
ISBN 978-1-338-60305-7
10 9 8 7 6 5 4   23 24 25 26 27
Printed in China   38
This edition first printing, July 2021

TABLE OF CONTENTS

....

Picture riddles fill this book;
Turn the pages! Take a look!

Use your mind, use your eye;
Read the rhymes and play **I SPY**!

....

I spy a magnet, a monkey, a mouse,
A squash, two flags, five 4s, a house;

A bird on a B, an exit sign,
A UFO, and a valentine.

I spy a rabbit, a rhyming snake,
An apple, a shark, and a birthday cake;

An unfinished word, a whale, two dimes,
Tic-tac-toe, and JUAN three times.

I spy an acorn, a cricket, a 3,
A shell in a nest, a shell from the sea;

Three feathers, two frogs, a ladybug, too,
Ten drops of water, and thread that is blue.

I spy a frog, a checkerboard 3,
A zigzag 4, and a zebra Z;

A rabbit, an arrow, a girl named DOT,
Six red blocks, and the missing knot.

I spy a marble, a clothespin clamp,
FUN, two keys, and a ruler ramp;

Three helmets, a hand, a hammer, a heart,
A checker, a chair, and a chalkboard chart.

I spy a schoolhouse, three camels, a bell,
A lighthouse, a swan, and a basket that fell;

A paintbrush, a drum, an upside-down block,
A calendar card, and a grandfather clock.

I spy a mail truck, a valentine cart,
A blue eyeball I, and a five-button heart;

Six arrows, two horses, two airplanes, two clocks,
A key, and a card that is in the wrong box.

I spy a chimney, an anthill, a 4,
A face with a smile, a star, and a score;

A feather, a twig, three footprints, a key,
A boat, two birds, a button, and BE.

The Stegosaurus ate plants for food.
Bobby C.

Stegosaurus walks on four legs and is my favorite dinosaur.
Rosa

Nobody knows what they are really like because they only have the bones.

This shows how big a stegosaurus is compared to a school bus.

Stegosaurus brain was only as big as a walnut.

Stegosaurus' tail spikes could

I spy a walnut, two turtles, a pail,
Two eggs that are hatching, a clothespin, a snail;

24

Ten pinecones, an ant, a shovel, a plane,
A little red star, three frogs, and a chain.

I spy a kickball, three ladders, and CLOCKS,
A small piece of chalk, four half-circle blocks;

A limo, a phone, and a rolling pin,
A flame, eight stars, and DEW DROP INN.

I spy three carrots, a magical hen,
Four keys, a candle, a cat, and a ten;

A teapot, a tin man, a rabbit asleep,
Anansi the Spider, and Little Bo Peep.

I spy a blender, a duck on a roll,
A pig, four bats, and a fishing pole;

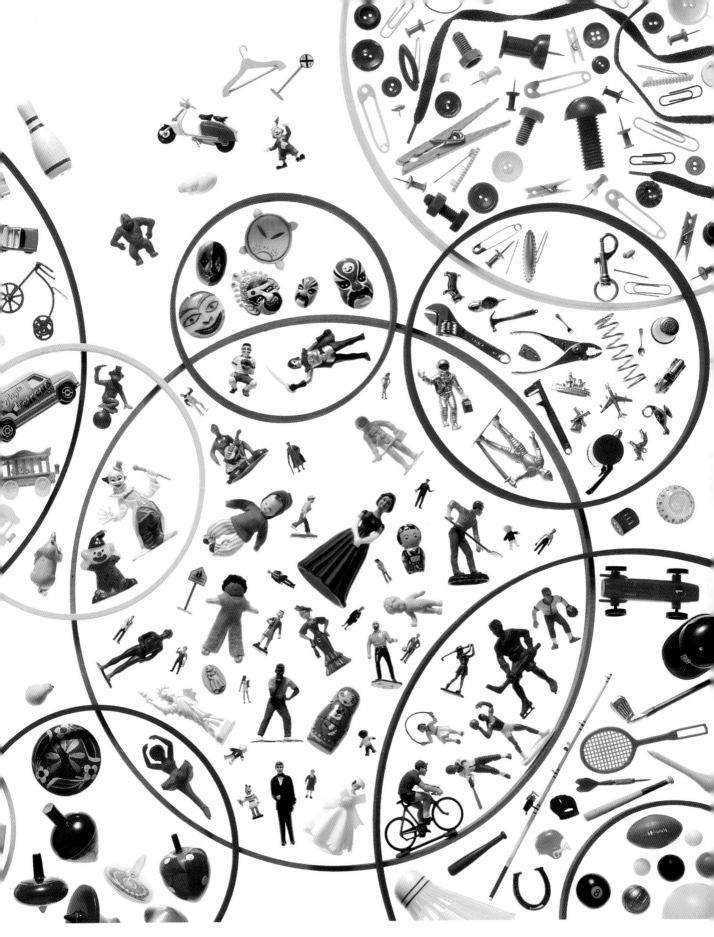

Five barrettes and five yellow rings,
And places for all of the outside things.

I spy a spider, an ice skate, a rake,
Two bracelets that match, a trumpet, a cake;

A dime, the Big Dipper, three flowerpots,
A coat with four buttons, and ten paper dots.

BONUS CHALLENGES

by Dan Marzollo and Dave Marzollo

"Find Me" Riddle

You'll need a sharp eye if you want to find me.
I'm in every picture. I'm a little striped _____.

There are still more riddles for you to complete.
Here is a challenge for readers to beat!

Every picture has a new set of clues.
Can you pick the right page to choose?

Find the Pictures That Go with These Riddles:

I spy a paperclip, three striped stones,
A kernel of corn, and three pinecones.

I spy a skate, a watering can,
An anchor, a pie, and an orange man.

I spy three bikes, a red tow truck,
Two jump ropes, a dog, and a duck.

I spy a giraffe, a horseshoe, a train,
Two dominoes, toast, and a tiny plane.

I spy 33, two pushpins, EGGS,
And a place where Rosa counted the legs.

I spy a ruler, a turtle shell,
A yellow fish, and SHOW + TELL.

I spy a duck, a bottle of glue,
The sun, and a snake that's red and blue.

I spy a helmet, a spool of thread,
Two marbles, glasses, and a vase that's red.

I spy six sheep, a mermaid's hair,
A moon, a bridge, and a teddy bear.

I spy a train, a little blue pail,
A duck, and a man delivering mail.

I spy a shoelace, five leaves that are brown,
A butterfly, a bike, a jack, and a frown.

I spy a birdhouse, a harp, a Z,
SMILE, three pigs, and a golden key.

I spy a ladder, a horse that rolls,
A racquet, and three triangular holes.

Write Your Own Picture Riddles

There are many more hidden objects and many more possibilities for riddles in this book. Write some rhyming picture riddles yourself, and try them out with friends.

How the I Spy Books Were Made

Jean Marzollo and Walter Wick together conceived the ideas for the photographs in *I Spy School Days*. Then Walter Wick created all the sets for *I Spy School Days* in his studio, photographing them with an 8" by 10" view camera. As much as possible, he used ordinary classroom materials and familiar objects from the environment so that readers who desire to make similar projects can do so. As the sets were constructed, Jean Marzollo and Walter Wick conferred by phone and fax on objects to go in the sets, selecting things for their rhyming potential, as well as their aesthetic, playful, and educational qualities. The final riddles were written upon completion of the photographs.

Special Acknowledgments

Again, we are grateful for the support and assistance of Grace Maccarone, Bernette Ford, Edie Weinberg, and many others at Scholastic. We also very much appreciate the help of Molly Friedrich at Aaron Priest Agency, Linda Cheverton-Wick, Elizabeth Woodson, Tina Chaden, Barbara Ardizone, Maria McGowan, Bruce Morozko, Frank and Ray Hills, Denis Gouey, Gator Laplante, and Lee Hitt. To Kevin Williams we extend a special thanks for his valuable and patient assistance throughout the entire *I Spy School Days* project.

Walter Wick and Jean Marzollo

Walter Wick is the award-winning photographer of the I Spy series as well as the author and photographer of the bestselling Can You See What I See? series. His other books include *A Ray of Light: A Book of Science and Wonder* and *A Drop of Water: A Book of Science and Wonder*. He has created photographs for books, magazines, and newspapers. Walter's photographs have been featured in museums around the United States. He lives with his wife, Linda, in Miami Beach, Florida.

More information about Walter Wick is available at walterwick.com and scholastic.com/canyouseewhatisee.

Jean Marzollo was the author of over a hundred books, including the bestselling I Spy series; *Help Me Learn Numbers 0–20*; *Help Me Learn Addition*; *Help Me Learn Subtraction*; and *I Am Water*; as well as books for parents and teachers, such as *The New Kindergarten*. Her sons, Dan and Dave, helped Jean write some of the newer I Spy books. Jean made sure that every riddle in every I Spy book was rich with concrete words that children could understand and that those words were set in an inviting pattern of rhythm and rhyme. For more information, go to scholastic.com/ispy.

Carol Devine Carson, the book designer, has designed covers for books by John Updike, Joan Didion, Alice Munro, and many more. For nineteen years, Marzollo and Carson produced Scholastic's kindergarten magazine, *Let's Find Out*.